HENRY AND MUDGE AND THE WILD GOOSE CHASE

The Twenty-Third Book of Their Adventures

Story by Cynthia Rylant
Pictures by Carolyn Bracken
in the style of Suçie Stevenson

READY-TO-READ
SIMON & SCHUSTER BOOKS FOR YOUNG READERS
New York   London   Toronto   Sydney   Singapore

THE HENRY AND MUDGE BOOKS

SIMON & SCHUSTER BOOKS FOR YOUNG READERS
An imprint of Simon & Schuster Children's Publishing Division
1230 Avenue of the Americas
New York, New York 10020
Text copyright © 2003 by Cynthia Rylant
Illustrations copyright © 2003 by Suçie Stevenson
All rights reserved, including the right of reproduction in whole or in part in any form.
SIMON & SCHUSTER BOOKS FOR YOUNG READERS is a trademark of Simon & Schuster.
READY-TO-READ is a registered trademark of Simon & Schuster, Inc.
Book design by Mark Siegel
The text for this book is set in 18-point Goudy.
The illustrations are rendered in pen-and-ink and watercolor.
Manufactured in the United States of America
10 9 8 7 6 5 4 3 2 1
Library of Congress Cataloging-in-Publication Data
Rylant, Cynthia.
Henry and Mudge and the wild goose chase : the twenty-third book of their adventures / story by Cynthia Rylant ; pictures by Suçie Stevenson.
p. cm. — (The Henry and Mudge books)
Summary: Henry and his dog Mudge tangle with a grumpy goose when they visit a farm.
ISBN 0-689-81172-1
[1. Domestic animals—Fiction. 2.Geese—Fiction. 3. Farm life—Fiction. 4. Dogs—Fiction.] I. Stevenson, Suçie, ill. II. Title. III. Series: Rylant, Cynthia. Henry and Mudge books.
PZ7.R982Heat 1999
[E]—dc21
98-7043
CIP
AC

Contents

Farm Fresh

One day Henry's mother told
Henry and Henry's father
that she wanted some
"farm-fresh eggs."

Henry imagined a plate full
of farm-fresh eggs.
"Yum," he said.
Mudge wagged.
He always wagged at "yum."

Then Henry's mother said
she wanted some
fresh-picked blueberries.
"Yum **yum**," said Henry.
Mudge wagged harder.
"Yum **yum**" was even better.

Then Henry's mother said
she wanted some sweet, fresh corn.
"Yum yum **yum**!" said Henry.
Mudge wagged so hard that
he knocked a chair over.

"Does this mean we're going
to a farm?" Henry asked his mother.
"I hope so," said Henry's dad.
He picked up the chair.
"One more yum and Mudge may
knock the whole house down."

"Wow!" said Henry. "We're going
to a farm, Mudge!"
Henry could hardly wait.

Welcome!

Henry and Mudge and Henry's parents
drove to the country.
They passed fields and barns.
They passed tractors and haystacks.

And once they had to stop
to let a duck and her children
cross the road.

Mudge wanted to get out of
the car and kiss the ducks.
But Henry wouldn't let him.
"No, Mudge," Henry said.
"No kisses."

Mudge kissed Henry instead.

Soon Henry's mother said,
"There's the sign!"
The sign said,
FRENCH'S FARM
2 MILES.
"Yay!" said Henry.

Henry's father drove up
to the farmhouse.
It was white and clean
and flowery.

"Look at those big sunflowers!"
said Henry.
"Everything is bigger in
the country," said Henry's mother.

They all got out of the car.
A woman wearing an apron
came from the house.
"Welcome!" she said. "I'm
Mrs. French."

20

Mrs. French was nice.
She told Henry he could walk
all around the farm.
She said that he could take Mudge.

While they explored,
Henry's parents would get eggs
and blueberries and corn
and all kinds of other
good farm things.

"Let's go, Mudge!" said Henry.
Mudge wagged and off they went.

The Chase

Henry and Mudge met a lot
of farm animals.
They met a goat that tried
to eat Henry's shirt.

25

They met chickens that
pecked Mudge's head.
(He didn't feel the pecks.
Mudge had a head like concrete.)

They met a shy cat and her kittens.

They met a sheep.

And then they met a goose.

"Uh-oh," said Henry.

"HONK!" said the goose.

"HONK! HONK! HONK!"

"Geese are very grumpy,"
Henry told Mudge.

"HONK! HONK! HONK!"

The goose was not happy
to see them.

He honked and honked and honked.
Mudge didn't like it.
He tried to hide between
Henry's legs.
"Yikes!" said Henry,
falling over.

The goose honked Henry and Mudge
all the way back
to the farmhouse.

They ran inside.
Henry's parents were paying
Mrs. French for the
bag of eggs and berries
and corn they were
taking home.

Henry's father looked
at Henry and Mudge.
He looked at the goose
honking outside the window.
"Looks like you've been
on a wild goose chase,"
he told Henry.

"Yes, but we weren't
doing the chasing!"
said Henry.

Mudge and the goose
looked at each other
through the window.
"Honk," said the goose.

Mudge looked.
"Honk," said the goose.
Mudge looked.
"Honk," said the goose.

36

"BARK!"

said Mudge.

37

The goose jumped three feet
in the air and went running
wildly away!

"You're right, Mom,"
Henry said, laughing.
"Everything **is** bigger in
the country.

Especially Mudge's **bark**!"
Mudge wagged proudly.
And Henry gave him
a farm-fresh kiss.